A NOTE TO PARENTS

Young children can be overwhelmed by their emotions--often because they don't understand and can't express what they are feeling. This, in turn, can frustrate parents. How can you help your child deal with a problem if the two of you don't even share a common vocabulary?

Welcome to **HOW I FEEL**--a series of books designed to bridge this communication gap. With simple text, lively illustrations, and an interactive format, each book describes familiar situations to help children recognize a particular emotion. It gives them a vocabulary to talk about what they're feeling, and it offers practical suggestions for dealing with those feelings.

Each time you read this book with your child you can reinforce the message with one of the following activities:

- Ask your child to make up a story about a little boy or girl who is angry.

- Make a list together of angry words--real or imaginary.

- Act out situations that spark your child's anger.

- Explore different emotions with the Make-a-Face activity card and reusable stickers included with this book.

I hope you both enjoy the **HOW I FEEL** series, and that it will help your child take the first steps toward understanding emotions.

Marcia Leonard

Executive Producers, JOHN CHRISTIANSON and RON BERRY
Art Design, GARY CURRANT
Layout Design, CURRANT DESIGN GROUP and BEST IMPRESSION GRAPHICS

ANGRY

by Marcia Leonard
illustrated by Bartholomew

This little boy broke his toy.
He feels angry.

This little girl is angry, too.
She wants to go out in the rain,
but her mom won't let her.

These two kids are angry at each other
because they both want to color
in the same book.

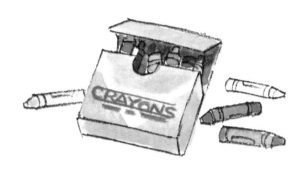

Do you ever get angry?
Can you make a face that looks angry?

This little girl is mad
because the big kids
won't let her play with them.

Does it make you mad
when someone says
you're too little to play?

These kids are upset because it's bedtime and they don't want to go to sleep yet.

Do you get upset when Mommy or Daddy wants you to go to bed?

This little boy is angry
because he feels left out.

Would that make you angry?

Sometimes talking to Mommy or Daddy about your anger makes you feel better.

Sometimes crying it out helps, too.

And sometimes all you need
is a big hug.

Anger can be scary.
That's because it's such a big,
strong feeling.

But the good thing is,
after a while, anger goes away.

MAKE-A-FACE
Instructions

Use this Make-a-Face activity to help your child identify and express a variety of emotions. Gently remove the page of reusable stickers from the center of this book. Let your child use the stickers to make faces on the blank card. Then talk about the faces. Are they angry, happy or sad? It's easy for your child to Make-a-Face--and fun too!